W9-CHS-648

The Little
Go-to-Sleep
Book

Juliet Harmer

A Margaret K. McElderry Book
Atheneum   1986   New York

For Lola

Library of Congress catalog card number: 85-71511
ISBN 0-689-50386-5
Copyright © 1985 by Juliet Harmer
All rights reserved
Printed in Belgium
First American Edition

Once upon a time
there was a little baby
who didn't like going to bed.
So every evening, the baby's
mother would say,

Listen, little one, everybody has to go to sleep.

Fish go to sleep
in little rockpools
in the sea.

Spiders go to sleep
down the plughole
in the bathtub.

Dogs go to sleep
in their baskets
by the fire.

This naughty pussycat is asleep on the table!

Frogs go to sleep
on wet lily leaves.

Horses go to sleep
standing in their stable.

Woodpeckers go to sleep
in a hole in the tree.

Mice go to sleep
in warm nests
under the floorboards.

Butterflies go to sleep
on the petals of a flower.

Sheep go to sleep
by the light of
the evening star.

Swans go to sleep
high up in the sky.

And little babies go to sleep
tucked up in their cradles.

Soon the little baby
was fast asleep.

Goodnight.